CAN'T SMURF

Peyo

Peyo

SCRIPT

SMURFS GRAPHIC NOVELS AVAILABLE FROM PAPERCUTZ™

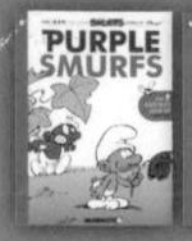

1. THE PURPLE SMURFS
2. THE SMURFS AND THE MAGIC FLUTE
3. THE SMURF KING
4. THE SMURFETTE
5. THE SMURFS AND THE EGG
6. THE SMURFS AND THE HOWLIBIRD
7. THE ASTROSMURF
8. THE SMURF APPRENTICE
9. GARGAMEL AND THE SMURFS
10. THE RETURN OF THE SMURFETTE
11. THE SMURF OLYMPICS
12. SMURF VS. SMURF
13. SMURF SOUP
14. THE BABY SMURF
15. THE SMURFLINGS
16. THE AEROSMURF
17. THE STRANGE AWAKENING OF LAZY SMURF
18. THE FINANCE SMURF
19. THE JEWEL SMURFER
20. DOCTOR SMURF
21. THE WILD SMURF
22. THE SMURF MENACE
23. CAN'T SMURF PROGRESS

- THE SMURF CHRISTMAS
- FOREVER SMURFETTE
- SMURFS MONSTERS
- THE VILLAGE BEHIND THE WALL

THE SMURFS graphic novels are available in paperback for $5.99 each and in hardcover for $10.99 each, except for THE SMURFS #21-#23, and THE VILLAGE BEHIND THE WALL, which are $7.99 in paperback and $12.99 in hardcover, at booksellers everywhere.
You can also order online at papercutz.com. Or call 1-800-886-1223, Monday through Friday, 9 – 5 EST. MC, Visa, and AmEx accepted. To order by mail, please add $4.00 for postage and handling for first book ordered, $1.00 for each additional book and make check payable to NBM Publishing. Send to: Papercutz, 160 Broadway, Suite 700, East Wing, New York, NY 10038.

THE SMURFS graphic novels are also available digitally wherever e-books are sold.

PAPERCUTZ.COM

CAN'T SMURF PROGRESS

"Can't Smurf Progress"
BY PEYO
WITH THE COLLABORATION OF
PHILIPPE DELZENNE AND THIERRY CULLIFORD FOR THE SCRIPT
LUDO BORECKI AND PASCAL GARRAY FOR ARTWORK,
AND NINE AND JOSE GRANDMONT FOR COLORS.

"Brainy Smurf's Walk"
BY PEYO
WITH THE COLLABORATION OF
ALAIN JOST FOR THE SCRIPT,
JEROEN DE CONINCK FOR ARTWORK,
PAOLO MADDELENI FOR COLORS.

Joe Johnson, *SMURFLATIONS*
Adam Grano/Dawn Guzzo, *SMURFIC DESIGNERS*
Janice Chiang, *LETTERING SMURFETTE*
Calvin Louie, *LETTERING ASSISTANT SMURF*
Matt. Murray, *SMURF CONSULTANT*
Dawn Guzzo, *SMURF COORDINATOR*
Jeff Whitman, *ASSISTANT MANAGING SMURF*
Jim Salicrup, *BRAINIER SMURF*

PAPERBACK EDITION ISBN: 978-1-62991-737-5
HARDCOVER EDITION ISBN: 978-1-62991-738-2

PRINTED IN CHINA JUNE 2017

Papercutz books may be purchased for business or promotional use. For information on bulk purchases please contact Macmillan Corporate and Premium Sales Department at (800) 221-7945 x5442.

DISTRIBUTED BY MACMILLAN
FIRST PAPERCUTZ PRINTING

CAN'T SMURF PROGRESS

Come on, be nice! If you go smurf me a mallet, I promise to smurf the repairs on your house!

Uh... that's very kind, but no thanks!... Hmm... Okay! Well, I'll go to Handy Smurf's to smurf it for you!

Smurfing me to do that! And a mallet, too! Such a heavy tool!
HEY! LAZY SMURF!
YAWN!

?!
Look out! You almost smurfed on our new toys!

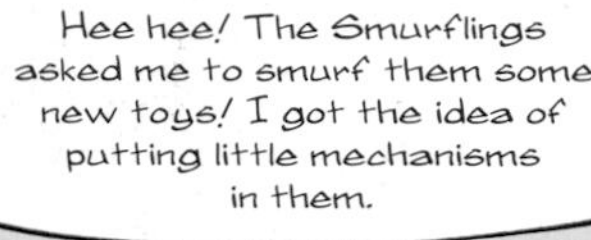
Hee hee! The Smurflings asked me to smurf them some new toys! I got the idea of putting little mechanisms in them.

You wind them up and, hup, they smurf all by themselves!
Oops! Look out, you can't stop progress!
?!
WAM

!!?!
!
Uh... say, Handy Smurf--

Could you smurf me something, too? You know, I get tired kind of fast, and--
?

After a few explanations...
You'll get what you asked for tomorrow! Meanwhile, don't forget to take Clumsy Smurf the mallet you came to smurf!
Oh, yeah! Hmm, I'd forgotten! Pfft!

?
Oof!
THUD
© Peyo 2

I'll never manage to smurf it! ⁘Pff!⁘
Wait! I may have a solution

So then, Lazy Smurf, are you walking your mallet?
Look out!! You forgot to smurf on its muzzle!
Great! Now I think they're making smurf of me!
HA! HA! HA!

The next day...
So, you wind up the smurf all the way, and the motor will do the rest! The levers are for going forward and maneuvering! That's it!
Oh, thank you, Handy Smurf!

Now, anyone can ask me for anything. I'll smurf it while resting!
?
RIKITIKITIKITIKITIKI

⁘YAWN!⁘ The clicking of this motor lulls... you... to sleep a little... Zzz...
RIKITIKITIKI

Rzzz
RIKITIKI

BING
BANG
CRAC
!

?!
LAZY SMURF?!
RIKITIKI
© Peyo

OUT WITH YOUR INFERNAL MACHINE!
Sorry, Baker Smurf!
RIKITIKITIKI
3

GOOD FOR NOTHING! SUNDAY SMURFER!
RIKITIKITIKI

Whoa! That looks so heavy, Carpenter Smurf! It makes me tired just watching you smurfing all those boards!
?
RIKITIK

Put them on the luggage-smurf! I'll smurf them wherever you like...

My goodness! Lazy Smurf working? Incredible!
KITIKITIKITIK

Hee hee hee! A walking sack of flour! Oh, no! There's a Smurf underneath! Hee hee!
RIKTIK

What? Someone's making fun of working Smurfs? Well, here's something that'll make you laugh!

WHUMP

Delivery address: Baker Smurf's shop! And get a smurf on!
RIKITIKITIKITIK

RIKITIKITIKITIKI
?

!
Gulp! I-- My brakes!
© Peyo 4

CRAC
BOOM
OUCH!

It's-- Uh-- The flour from Miller Smurf... I-- the brakes-- Uh... Boom!... Heh heh! Hmm!

Smurfing all
the flower with
a strainer! That Baker
Smurf is smurfly
harsh...
This machine seems
smurfly practical to me after all.
I'll ask Handy Smurf to smurf me one
to deliver my bread...
Yes, I'm
interested in
that, too...
Let's go
see Handy
Smurf...

Hmm! Okay then! I'll see
what I can smurf for you...
Come back tomorrow!
Cool!
Thanks,
Handy Smurf!

And the next morning...
Smurftastic!
Let's get to
work!

Pastries,
croissants, loaves of bread!
Fresh and hot!
DING
DILING
Yum!
This way,
Baker
Smurf!

What
service!
Yum...
Good morning,
Greedy Smurf.
Bon appétit!
Hee hee
hee!
DING
DING DING

That evening...
I did gain a little
time on delivery, but I still
have so many things to
smurf! Pfff...

Unless...

Handy
Smurf could surely
smurf me this
little favor!

BANG
POW

You two, again?!
Yes! Ow! I was going to Handy Smurf's!
Oh, you, too?

Smurf you some machines that'll smurf your work for you? Hmm!
Yes! No more labor and a life of plenty for us! Let the machines do the work!
A Smurf isn't made for smurfing!
I couldn't have put it better myself!

Okay! I'm just the Smurf you need! But I'll need your help!

The following days, the Smurfs spent all their time building machines that would completely upend their lives...

And so, one fine morning...
There! One more little adjustment and the breadsmurfer will be ready!
Awesome, Handy Smurf! I'll go see how Miller Smurf's doing!

This conveyor belt is awesome! It smurfs the flour directly from the mill to my bakery!

Ah! He's already smurfing the wheat!
RRRRRRR

HEY! BA-A-A-KER SMU-RF! THIS MA-MACHINE IS SU-SUPERSMURF!
RRRRRRR

I smurfed the harvest from my wheat field in less than an hour! I just have to smurf it into the mouth of my mill now!
CLAC
CLAC
© Peyo

And hup!

And now the wo--
?!
?
CLAC
CLAC

LOOK OUT!
HEY!

OH, NO! THE MILL SMURFED MILLER SMURF WHOLE!
AYE! YI! YI!
TCHIKATCHIKATCHIC

?!
TCHIKATCH
CHIC

HA! HA! HA! The smurf's in the bag!

Get me out of here instead of smurfing like a fool!

You must be careful! These machines can be smurfy dangerous!
Absolutely! Just imagine! I could've found you in my toast for breakfast! Yuck!

The breadsmurfer's ready to go, Baker Smurf! The honor's all yours for turning it on!

There! All the ingredients have been smurfed in! Just a pinch of salt, and--

Hmpf!... Here goes!
© Peyo
7

TCHOOF TCHOOF
BROLOBOM BODOM
BROOF
CREEEEETCH
TOOOOOT
PSHEEEEE
BLOM PROTCH
BROL ROLL ROLL ROLL ROLL ROLL
IT'S-- IT'S SMURFING!

TING
WOKKAWOKKA

Hee hee! It smells delicious! Oops! It's still hot!
Go ahead, taste it!

Crunch! Crunch! Crunch! Gulp!
Well?

Delicious! You smurf this fresh bread! My treat!

TING WOKKA WOKKA TING TING
TING TING WOKKAWOKKAWOK
WOKKAWOKKAWOKKA
TING
!
?
CREAK CREAK

And enough for the whole village in one go! Hurray, Handy Smurf!
HURRAY!
8

The next morning...

It's five o'clock. The village is awakening...
...And our work is already smurfed!

Let's go find Carpenter Smurf and smurf it easy under the big oak!

So, how's it smurfing?
This invention of Handy Smurf's is incredible! Look what I can smurf!

ROLROLLROLL
PING
CLING CLANG
ROLL ROLL

!
?
VRRR
ZEEE TCHAC
BROOF
DZEEEEE
TCHOF
TCHAC TCHAC
POC
BROOT
BROOT

RRRRRRR

Wow! What quality! You couldn't have smurfed better yourself!
Uh, hmm! Let's not exaggerate...

So? Satisfied?
Oh, yes! You're awesome!
You deserve a statue!
TCHAC ZEEEEEEE
BROOT
BROOT ZEEEEEEE
VRRRRRR
POC TCHAC
©Peyo

Later...
Have you already finished your work?
No, no! We have machines that smurf our work for us!
And they never get tired! Hee hee hee!

Well, I never! I'm going to go smurf the others! We have the right to rest, too!

The news spreads rapidly...

I want a machine that smurfs my dishes!
And me, one that washes my smurfs!
And I want a sewing machine!
I want one that peels my onions! Sniff! ...
Me, I don't like sniffs!
!

Handy Smurf starts working day and night! Soon, dozens of machines emerge from his workshop and invade the village...
I promise! I won't play the trumpet anymore!
?

One morning...
KLAK

PWAT

PWAAT

That alarm is brutal, but smurfly effective! Okay, let's get up!
CLONG

Oops! Hee hee hee!
ZOOF
DOING
© Peyo

HUP!
PLOP

A hearty, little breakfast will smurf me going for the whole day! Yum yum!
10

* See: "The Clockwork Smurf" in THE SMURFS #11 "Smurf Soup."

You're polluting the air with the noise your cursed engines smurf!
?
SQUEEKSQUEEEKSQUEEEEK

Look! My firefly is very sensitive to the noise! She's flashing non-stop! All your smurferies are making the poor thing sick!

And also, it's not good for growing my vegetables!
Now you're exaggerating!

I'll go smurf elsewhere, where I can still hear my beans smurfing! Good-bye!

But you can't smurf the village like that, while Papa's Smurf's away! What's more, I'll tell him when he--

INCREDIBLE!
FANTASTIC!
?

Here are the servants who will smurf at our service day and night!
That's mind-smurfing, Handy Smurf!

My dear Smurfs, today, we're entering a new era--

Me, I don't like errors...
12

On this historic day, this little click will be a great leap ahead for the Smurf world!

CLIK

Well what?!
It doesn't smurf!
?

Bah! I was sure of it! A wooden smurf that smurfs by itself... Ha! Ha! Ha! That's a good one! Ridiculous!

POW
!?

Hee hee hee! Bravo! It understood right away what we expected from it!
Ha ha ha!
CLAP CLAP

CLIC CLAC
CLONG
CLAP
CLIC
CLOC

TCHIKETTATCHIKETTATCHIKETTA
TCHIC TCHIC TCHIC

Aye- yi-yi! It's going to bust its smurf!

BANG

For smurf-wrench's sake!
TCHIC CHIC TCHIKETTA
TIC
POC POC POC
13

I don't understand. It should smurf!
SCRITCH SCRATCH

Unless... What's that smurf there?

Uh... Heh heh!... It's my screwdriver! I thought I'd smurfed it somewhere!

?
CLAP
DOING

PLUNK
CRIC TCHIK TENG
TIC
PLING

POM
KWIT
BLIP

Smurf me a hot chocolate and a smurf baba, please!
?
CLANG
CLONG

!
?!
!
!

HURRAY FOR HANDY SMURF!
COOL!
BRAVO!
AWESOME!
© Peyo

HOT CHOCOLATE FOR EVERYONE! ON ME!
YIPPEE!
14

A little later...
And next, smurf two little touches of white on him there in the shape of a bowtie!
Oh, yes, that's stylish, Vanity Smurf! Thanks to your advice and my painting talents, we'll give these tree trunks a nice look!
CLIK
HEY, WAITER!

I'd like you to smurf me a few cookies and some strawberry juice, please!
BLIP

Oh, what quick service! Here! Smurf your tray there!

Yum! Hey! Look! It's smurfing! Yum, *crunch*-- Pull in the line!

Good catch! *Gulp!*

Another nice piece for my-- *crunch*-- Collection!

DING DILING
Oh! That's coming from Smurfette's! Smurf there fast, she probably needs your help!
TWEET BIP

At last! Where were you? Hurry up, there's more laundry to smurf!
BLIP
© Peyo 15

And afterwards, smurf my back with the suntan oil...

That servant is lucky, isn't it?!
Yes, but that's enough now!

Hey! We need you to smurf ball!

What about my legs?!
Later, Smurfette, later! We have to exercise to stay in shape...

Yeah! Well smurfed!
PUNT
Go ahead, smurf me the ball!

Five minutes later...
Okay! Enough smurfing! Playing sports is tiring...
That smurfs me an appetite! Hey, you! Go smurf the cart!

There's nothing like a good meal to resmurf your strength after all that exercise...
Hmm...
16

Not content with simply becoming lazy, the Smurfs become ever more demanding...
This plate was badly smurfed! I still see a stain here!

And I have fingerprints on my glass!
Gross!

I don't even have any silverware!
Scandalous!

What has that clockwork cook smurfed us that's good?
No idea, it's a surprise!
Me, I don't smurf! So long as it smurfs...
Menu

It's not hot enough!
It's too hot!

GLUG GLUG

No! Smurf me another jug! There are too many bubbles in this one!

Everyone ends up being happy all the same...
Mmm... Not bad after all.
It's almost better even than Chef Smurf's grub!

DINGALING
17

Me, I don't like eating with others! But I do like strawberry juice! Here, fill my glass!
CLIK

A few moments later...
In fact, I don't like strawberry juice! I'd rather have raspberry juice! Go smurf me one!
CLAK
?

I don't like raspberry juice, after all! So smurf me blueberry juice!
!?

TCHIKKA
TCHIC

You know, I'm not thirsty at all! What's more, I don't like being thirsty!
CLONK

TCHOOF
BURP
PLUNK
CLIK
CLONG
CLAP

?!
?
BLOING

You overdo it, Grouchy Smurf! You even manage to drive a mechanical smurf up the wall! It's completely out of order!

CLIK
CLAK
Me, I don't like these mechanical smurfs! They smurf down over nothing and that makes me tired!
© Peyo
18

Smurfette is taking her shower outside! This is a chance not to be missed! And nobody knows this spot from which you can see everything!

But-- You've already smurfed half of the supper...
Uh-hmm! Yes! I was starting-- Yum to get smurfily hungry...

Bu-- Uh-- I saved this little apple for you, Smurfette. Here--
OH! You glutton!

The servants don't get a moment's rest...
No, no! You're smurfing everything backwards! Wait, I'll sing it to you! Listen closely!

LALAAA LALILALAA

They endure everything without complaint...
And after this moral treatise, let's smurf a few Smurf maxims...

Mmmyes... This smurf baba is a success! Smurf a hundred of them for me by tomorrow.

Smurf the sky in azure blue! Afterwards, you'll smurf a light touch of yellow here. Finish it for tomorrow and I'll sign it!

And at nightfall, when the Smurfs go to bed...
Hey! Smurf me a second pillow!
A glass of water!
My back is itching! Come scratch me!
My hanky!
Snuff the candle!
Bring me my book of proverbs, I'll smurf a few pages before I fall asleep...
20

The next day...

Once the trash is collected, the servant displays a curious behavior...
HIC HIC HOC

PSHHHHHH

ROLOBROLOBOM
?
!?

PLOP

Oh, my! It swallows the trash and smurfs bricks out of them!
Bricks?!

It should make chocolate bars instead... Slurp!

A little later, but much higher up...

Ah! It's so pleasant to get back to the quiet of our village...

What... what is all of this smurfiness?!
TCHIKETTA

Where have all the Smurfs gone?

?!?

Oh! Papa Smurf's back!
Hello, Papa Smurf!
Come smurf down with us! It's really nice smurfing here!
Hey, you! Something to drink for Papa Smurf!
!

Can someone explain to me what's smurfing on here?

Uh-- It's-- It's because of Handy Smurf, Papa Smurf! At first, he smurfed some machines that did our daily tasks in our place!...

Then, we asked him to smurf us some smurf servants to be at our service day and night! Thanks, go smurf me some ice!

Now we have the real life of smurf! Yep!

Well done! Are you proud of yourselves?! Just look at you!
!
?!
?

So, the lessons of the past haven't--
!?
© Peyo
23

For me? Uh-- Thanks!

Hey?! What are you-- Careful! That's smurfly fragile!

G-Gently... Gently...

?
Laborator

!
No Smurfing
GUNPOWDER

Oh, my. Never has my laboratory been so clean and well-smurfed.
And... Concerning the mechanical smurfs, what must we smurf?

Uh...We'll smurf about that later... For now, I'm going to rest, because I'm very tired from my trip...
24

A few days later...
I'll take advantage of what the servants smurfed to my lab to put away these dangerous potions...

They'll be safer in the attic.

Papa Smurf, come quick, we need you!
?

It can't wait five minutes?
No, no, it's urgent!
Laboratory

Fine! Hey, you! Once you've finished what you're smurfing, go smurf this in my attic! And be very careful...
BLIP?

Papa Smurf is unaware that what he's done will have grave consequences...

PLISH
PLASH

CLING
BLING
DZING

That's when the mixture of the different substances has a strange reaction...
BROOOOOO?
PLAP

WOOF
PTOIIING
25

GRRR...

Rhaaa... Eat more trash!
?

So, now that one's starting to talk! If I weren't so tired, I'd go tell Papa Smurf...

Bothering me to show me that the mechanical smurfs could replace them at the springtime festival dance! Those slackers are starting to get on my smurfs!

Oh! At least there's one doing his job correctly!

Thank you, Smurf Servant!
KRRPPT ?

Meanwhile...
Get a move on, you slacker, or you'll get a taste of my stick!
?

Smurf not hit servant!
?

You, trashcan, what do I smurf? After all, it's only a machine!

NOT HIT SERVANT!
© Peyo 26

Why obey Smurf? No let be pushed around!

BZZZzzzz

The talking trashcan?! Are you sure of what you're smurfing?
I--I assure you, Papa Smurf!

It was here and it was very angry! Look, even my servant has disappeared!

Hmmm... It's a bit late to smurf anything at all today! We'll see about it tomorrow!

Unfortunately, Papa Smurf won't have time, because that night...
Har! Har! Har! Trashcan change machines ...

And servants never obey Smurfs again! Har! Har! Har!

At daybreak...
Yaaawn! A nice breakfast in bed!

DING
DILING

They're taking their time smurfing breakfast today!

Later...
Well, is it coming?!
DING
DELING
DILING
DELING

I'll smurf him to ignore Brainy Smurf!
© Peyo 27

Hey! You!
You don't answer
the smurf bells any
longer?!
?
SNAP

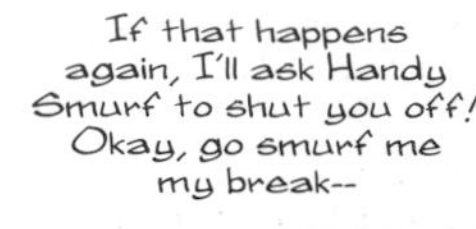

If that happens
again, I'll ask Handy
Smurf to shut you off!
Okay, go smurf me
my break--

POW
krpow!

There,
last Smurf! Go on
then! With the others!
Har! Har! Har!

Did you see, Papa Smurf?!
All the servants have gone
bonkers! They smurfed
everyone first thing
this morning.
Z

Yes, they didn't
even leave me time to smurf on
something decent!
TILT
SLURP

Clearly, the trashcan is their
leader! I wonder what could have
smurfed him life and speech...

Yesterday's
when he
started to talk,
just after he
smurfed your
trash. I
saw him...

But... I didn't smurf any
trash yesterday. For Smurf's
sake! My dangerous
potions!
?
28

Now, Trashcan become King of Servants! Servants no longer serve Smurfs! Smurfs serve servants! Smurfs serve Trashcan!

HAR! HAR! HAR!
SLAM

They're going to enslave us! I don't even know how to work anymore...
What will become of us?

We must neutralize the clockwork trashcan! Once he can't do any harm, it'll be easy for us to resmurf control of the other servants.

Help me smurf up to that skylight. I'll try to reach my laboratory...

Be careful, Papa Smurf...
BOP
BIP

If I can reach that branch, I'll be able to smurf easily to my laboratory...

?

?!
SPLOOSH

PLOP

29

Lock Old Smurf in prison in forest!
Old?! A little respect, please!

Well?
Papa Smurf got smurfed! They're taking him out of the village!

Old Smurf hostage! Smurfs no run away again! OBEY! Build house for me in village!

OBEY! BUILD PALACE FOR KING TRASH!
HAR! HAR! HAR!

The next morning, the Smurfs are put to work...
© Peyo 30

No kidding around with that one, he's mean!
And what's more, he has stinky smurf!

Some must pick up the trash...
SCHTICK

...in order to feed King Trash's insatiable hunger...

...which produces bricks at a sustained pace...
THUD

At night, the Smurfs are locked away in their homes....
BAM BAM BAM
CLIK KLAK
SNIF!

A few days later, a dark silhouette looms over the village...

And it's with great pomp that King Trash takes possession of his new palace...

OBEY! KING ME! FINALLY! GREAT PALACE FOR ME. TRASH THE FIRST! AT LAST! KING ME!
© Peyo 31

Bah! Now that he has his palace, at least he'll smurf us in peace! We won't have to work anymore!

NOW, SMURFS SERVE, SMURFS CLEAN! GO! OBEY!

Later...
Clean, clean... ÷kof, kof÷... Nice maids we make! I'm going to smurf an allergy from all this dust!
ACHOO ACHOO

?
RUB RUB

!
CLAP CLAP

What an obsessive servant!
RUB RUB

Me? Wash that?! Never!

How humiliating! That trashcan will pay for this!

And at nightfall, the Smurfs are led back home...

Their future is entirely uncertain...
32

I wonder what Greedy Smurf's smurfing right now...? He must be busy stuffing himself with cakes...

Good ol' Greedy Smurf!

And Jokey Smurf with his gifts... I'd gladly open one now!

And Smurfette... Golly! The beautiful Smurfette!

And Lazy Smurf who's no smurf at all... And Papa Smurf and his little ol' experiments...

I even miss Brainy Smurf! He'd start smurfing at me, and I'd toss a cabbage at his head! Ha! Ha! Ha!

SIGH!

How could I believe I could smurf without them?! I'm going back, for Smurf's sake!
33

Some time later...
The Smurf Village! It hasn't changed at all!

Yes, it has! What's that funny-looking tower? No doubt another smurfidity of Handy Smurf's

BLIP
?
CRAC

What's that smurfing out there by itself? Weird! Yep, let's follow it!

!?

A prison?!

Blooming zucchinis! Papa Smurf!

?
CLIK
KLAK

KRRPT!
© Peyo
34

My poor, little Smurfs! What fix have they gotten us into again? How will we get out of this?
YUM YUM

?
BOP

PSSSST
?

!
BIP

Pssssst, Papa Smurf!
?!
Golly, gee smurf! Is the old bat deaf or what?!

Ahem! The old bat will act like he didn't hear a thing!
Uh...Sorry, Papa Smurf, it's just that--

It's fine, it's fine, Farmer Smurf! How did you manage to escape the village?
It's a long story, Papa Smurf...

?

KRRPT

BLIP?

I must free Papa Smurf! But I'll never manage by myself...

I have to get help from the village!
© Peyo
35

Later, at the village outskirts...
There are mechanical smurfs everywhere! This won't be easy...

How can I smurf there without being spotted?!

Soon after...

BRING ME SMURF WHO'S HANDY!

King Trash very lonely! Handy build queen for me! You have two days to do! Go! Obey!
36

YOU, THERE!
!

Take Handy to his workshop!
Yes... Uh... Blpt...Hmm... Prrrt...

Grmbl...

Hey! I'm telling you my workshop's that way, you stupid block of wood!

Okay, okay! I get it! No need to smurf me kicks!
Shhhhhh!
PUNT
PUNT

Handy Smurf, it's me, Farmer Smurf! Golly, gee smurf!
?

Farmer Smurf?! Give me a hug, old buddy!

POW

Gracious, Handy Smurf, you've got to help me smurf Papa Smurf! He's smurfed in a prison smurfed by one of those horrible machines and, all alone, I couldn't smurf him out of harm's way, so I smurfed myself inside that piece of wood to smurf help from the village on the sly, and--

Whoa! Whoa! Okay! I got it! Calm down!

Let's go! I have a little idea how to smurf that diabolical machine...

Later, in the forest...

♫
?

!
SHPLIITZZ

Let's hope he'll smurf into the slipknot...

ZWIP
¿

ZOOM

Golly gee, your trap smurfed well! Weren't that a mite violent, Handy Smurf?!
Uh... I didn't plan on that part.

Let's take him down and see where he smurfed the key to the prison!
38

It's a catasmurfre! He doesn't have the key on him!

Papa Smurf! Papa Smurf! We smurfed the mechanical smurf who was guarding you...
...But we didn't smurf any key!

Hmmmm... King Trash is probably keeping it on himself!

If I had my tools, I could smurf the lock...

Darned, blasted door!
THWAK

?
POOF

!?!

Oh, my! What smurfed to it? The door smurfed into dust!

It's termites! Look! All the wood got smurfed and is as fragile as cardboard!

Thank you, my little Smurfs!
Papa Smurf! Gracious!
© Peyo

Tonight, we'll quietly go to my laboratory...
39

That night, strange bushes slip into the village...

Shhh! Don't make any noise!

It's-- it's a catasmurfre!

Everything's been smurfed!

Later, after a methodical search...
Okay then! There's no miracle solution... But there must surely be a way to smurf those cursed piles of wood...

To smurf those **PILES OF WOOD...** Golly gee! Yes, of course!
SNAP

THE TERMITES! Remember they smurfed your prison door, Papa Smurf!

Farmer Smurf, you're smurftastic!
Yes, but... How do we smurf them to the mechanical smurfs?

Wait! I think I've smurfed the solution! Listen...

We're going to smurf to the workshop, and there, we-- whisper, whisper, and don't smurf your eyes trying to read what's being said...
40

Two days later...
AAAH! MY QUEEN!
Trash the First has finally become a real king! Tonight, feast for all! Except for Smurfs! Har! Har! Har!

That evening, in King Trash's fortress...
Wah-ha! Ha! Smurfs funny! Aren't they, my queen?!
RAP RAP
Grmbl!
GLING
DING
DING
DING
TING
GLING
GLING
DING
DING
DING
BLING

?

Hmm! Queen not talk much! No fun...
YUM!
SCHLORP
GULP
BURP
CRUNCH

Meanwhile, in the village...
Papa Smurf, you escaped?!
Hurry, we must free the others!

Queen not eat? Trash no good?
NOK NOK

41 © Peyo
?
CRRR
CRRR
CRRR
CRRR
CRRR
CRRR

CRAC
?!

RHAAA!

!

?

?
KRPPT?
CRAC
CRIC
CRRRR
CROC
TUMP

KRASH

Little bugs eat wood! Eat servants! Betrayed by Smurf who's handy! Put them in queen!

King Trash not stay here, or else--

For the clockwork Smurfs, it's a massacre...
SPRRITZZ
© Peyo
42

Outside...
Heave... Ho! Come on! A little more effort!
Smurf it here, against this stone!

Are you sure about what you're doing, Handy Smurf?
Trust me, Papa Smurf!

Har! Har! Har! King Trash run away and come back for revenge!

Surrender, you cursed trashcan! Your reign is over!
!

NEVER!

Ha! My secret way out!

HAR! HAR! HAR!

HEY! Where me be?
© Peyo

Go ahead, Handy Smurf! Put your machine to work!

TCHIC
TCHAC
POP DZEEEEEE
VRRRRRR
43

VRRR
ZEEEEE
TCHAC
BROOM
DZEEEE
TCHAC TCHAC
POC
RRR
RRRRR
ZZZZZ
BROOT
BROOT
YIPPEE!
It's been smurfed into wooden things!

YAHOOOO!
Hurray for Papa Smurf! Hurray for Handy Smurf! Hurray for Farmer Smurf!

A few days later...
It's good to resmurf some healthy physical activity, isn't it, Hefty Smurf?
You're telling me, Handy Smurf!

And to think we were saved by termites... Unbelievable!
Oh, yeah! Without them, we'd have been smurfed for sure!
Later!

WAK
CRAK

Cursed bugs!

Darn! My ladder!
?
Me, I don't like termites!
Oh, no! Not my bed!
?
Hee hee! Golly!
END

GRRR...
ME HATE SMURFS! ME GET REVENGE!

WATCH OUT FOR PAPERCUTZ™

Welcome to the tyranny-filled, trash-talking, twenty-third SMURFS graphic novel by Peyo, from Papercutz, the small gang of renegade robotic humanoids dedicated to publishing great graphic novels for all ages. I'm Jim Salicrup, your half-awake Smurf-in-Chief, here to make a couple of BIG ANNOUNCEMENTS!

The first BIG ANNOUNCEMENT is that we're publishing a Smurfs graphic novel at virtually the same time it's being published in Europe! That's because it features characters from the all-new, fully-animated Smurfs movie from Sony Animation. For years Papercutz has been playing catch-up with the original SMURFS graphic novels that have been regularly published in Europe for nearly 60 years! We've more or less have been publishing THE SMURFS in the same chronological order as they were originally published in Europe. But we decided to make an exception this time and leap ahead to the present to bring you this new exciting graphic novel, "The Village Behind the Wall," which features the new Smurfs introduced in the new Smurfs movie! Check out "Brainy Smurf's Walk," starting on the very next page! (Did I mention that it's new?)

The second BIG ANNOUNCEMENT is that Papercutz is launching a whole new line of graphic novels, filled with exciting characters, a big dose of romance, and great writing and artwork. The new line of titles is called Charmz, and we suspect you're going to love each and every Charmz title because they're totally irresistible! You can find out a lot more about Charmz by going to papercutz.com, but to whet your appetite for what's coming up, we're featuring a short preview of STITCHED #1 "The First Day of the Rest of Her Life," starting right after "Brainy Smurf's Walk" in the pages ahead.

In the meantime don't forget about the previous 22 SMURFS graphic novels, not to mention BENNY BREAKIRON, PUSSYCAT, THE SMURFS & FRIENDS, and THE SMURFS ANTHOLOGY, all available at booksellers everywhere, as well as the smurfiest libraries. But let me give you fair warning—just when you think you've caught up with all the SMURFS graphic novels, we'll publish another one! Hey, it's what we do!

Smurf you later,

Jim

STAY IN TOUCH!

EMAIL:	salicrup@papercutz.com
WEB:	papercutz.com
TWITTER:	@papercutzgn
INSTAGRAM:	@papercutzgn
FACEBOOK:	PAPERCUTZGRAPHICNOVELS
FANMAIL:	Papercutz, 160 Broadway, Suite 700, East Wing, New York, NY 10038

BRAINY SMURF'S WALK

When the Smurfs and the girls meet one another for the first time, there's an awkward, distrustful moment...

They observe and criticize one another...

Then curiosity wins out...

Someone takes the first step...

What? They're going off with Brainy Smurf?
Very weird!

Uh, yes... They noticed my superiority right away!

A superior smurfache, yes!
They're going to kick themselves for inviting him.

We have tons and tons of activities. We never get bored! And how do you smurf your days in your village?

Well... Often, there's work to be smurfed. We repair the bridge or the dam. Or else, we go smurf fruits and berries in the forest...

And we love to smurf parties. We eat, sing, and dance the whole evening!
Oh, yeah, us, too!

Show us how you all dance!
Certainly!

Here goes. I smurf myself into position.

Tralalaaa smurflala...

Tralalaaa...

Smurf-lalaaaaa!
Ah, okay... Not terrible!
2

Come on, girls! It's our turn to smurf him a demonstration.
Yeaaah! I'll run and get my instrument!

Ready? Here goes!

Okay, come dance with us!
Uh... I don't think I--

Whoa! Ouch!

I don't think he has a knack for our dancing!
Oww! My neck! My back!
Don't you smurf! We'll look after it!

Come in, I'll take care of you.

Smurf onto the table. Come on, don't be afraid!

First, some essential vine oil... It's excellent for your joints!
Oh! That smurfs!... I mean, it has a strong odor!
3

And now, the most effective thing...
A massage?

No, I'm going to smurf our sucker beetle on your back!
AAAH!

No reason to! I feel much better!
Well, his cure was smurfly fast!

We also smurf a lot of exercise. Do you want to try?
No, thanks! Not at the moment!

Then, could we go smurf a walk in the forest?
Yes, that's a good idea!

To smurf for our outings, we always take our bows and arrows.

They're for defending ourselves. If someone attacks us, we knock out our adversary. Heeheehee!

Like this; look!

ZING

POK

Not bad! I'm a champion, too, at bow and arrows!
Show us!
4

Wow!
What style!

OWW!
BAP

Who smurfed that arrow?

Smurfstorm's the one who got smurfed!
The way she is, you'd better run fast, champ! Heeheehee!
M-my glasses were fogged up!
Why yes, of course!

Now, let's go smurf on your camouflage!
What?

Yes, you saw: we never go out without camouflage.
Everything you need is here!

I could see him with this one.
It's a little small!

Ah, look... This one will do the job!
Nice!
Is this really necessary?

Absolutely, it's a security measure. Don't move, I'll put your glasses back on.
It's perfect like that!

Wait, wait! Let's smurf an original touch...
5

Yes! You made a great smurf with that!
It's awesome!

But I can't go out like this!
And why not? It looks smurf on you!

Just wait long enough for us to camouflage ourselves, too, and we'll go!

Let's go!

Oh! Look at that!

Brainy Smurf! We didn't recognize you...
You're looking smurfly good in that outfit!
Keep moving, keep moving! No dragging around!
?

To smurf in the forest, we'll set out from up there.

From here? But how--?
Easy, you just smurf from vine to vine.
You'll see, it's really smurf!
6

Hup, we're off!

YIPPEE!

Uh, yes... Yippee!

Heeheehee!
And whoahooo!

And whoa--

AAAAAHH
Oh, he fell!

Don't you smurf, everything's okay This plant broke my fall!
Ah, yes... That's good for the fall. But that plant is a smurfulus with stinging hairs.

A WHAT?

Yikes! Oww! It burns! Smurf me out of here!
We're coming!

You're better off on solid ground!
7

Later, at the village...

A special preview of STITCHED #1 "The First Day of the Rest of Her Life" by Mariah McCourt and Aaron Alexovich

---WHAT---
AM I?

CRIMSON....
DON'T BE AFRAID...
---FOLLOW ---THE---
LIGHTS---
WAIT!
WAIT FOR ME! DON'T GO! I--

OH. WOW.
I THINK I WAS BORN TODAY.
THE ONLY THINGS I KNOW ARE MY NAME...

...AND THAT I HAVE ABSOLUTELY NO IDEA OF WHERE I AM OR WHERE I SHOULD GO...
CAW
CEMETERY OF ASSUMPTIONS
SLAM
YIKES!
YEEEKS!

MY LEGS FEEL WEIRD.
LIKE THEY DON'T REMEMBER HOW TO RUN--
BOO
BOO
AWOOOO
OOF!
AWWOOOOoooooOOOOOooo
≶PANT≶ ≶PANT≶ NEED TO... HIDE...
HELP!
LET ME IN!
HELP!
--HELP?
AWOOOOOOOooo